A COMPILATION OF SHORT STORIES

Wayne J. Zywicki

NEWMAN SPRINGS PUBLISHING
320 Broad Street
Red Bank, NJ 07701

First originally published by Newman Springs Publishing 2024

ISBN 979-8-89308-904-2 (Paperback)
ISBN 979-8-89308-905-9 (Digital)

Printed in the United States of America

Introduction

The following collection of short stories is the result of a bad case of *foot-in-mouth* derived from a job interview.

I had just completed a twenty-year hitch in Uncle Sam's Navy and decided to travel the good old USA. Having to pay for my room, board, and travel expenses diminished my funds in very short order. It was time to look for gainful employment.

Among the various questions asked during the interview was whether I could read blueprints. Never having had a problem in this department, I answered in the affirmative. The interviewer told me it was hard to find someone who could read blueprints and hired me on as a journeyman. I informed him I never had a problem unless he had some kind of special prints. He informed me they were standard shop prints and opened up a set. I had never seen blueprints with so many lines and symbols.

At this point, I knew I was way over my head; however, my ego trumped common sense, causing me to keep my mouth shut. Following my interview, I headed straight for the community college in Stockton, California, and signed up for a blueprint reading course. My plan, such as it was, was to fake any problems I had during the day and bring the prints to my instructor in the evening. Fortunately, I was assigned to work with a journeyman who knew how to read prints, which ended the crisis.

A couple of months later, the company folded, placing me back in the unemployment line. It was time for brainstorm number two. Since I was already taking a half course of six units, I decided to enroll for the full twelve units and file for school aid under the GI Bill.

I enrolled in various subjects, two of which were English and creative writing. To plagiarize Paul Harvey, "And now you know the rest of the story."

A Day in Moscow

On the fourth stop of the Scandinavian cruise, the ship entered the port of St. Petersburg for a two-night stay in Russia. This gave Wade the opportunity for two tours. Day one would be a flight to Moscow, and day two, a city tour of St. Petersburg.

Russian immigration had tables set up at the gangway. Once the agents determined we weren't trying to enter Russia illegally (like what person in his or her right mind would), the tour group of four-hundred-plus boarded the buses for transportation to the airport. The one-hour flight to Moscow took almost one and a half hours, but they made it safely, and that's all that counts.

The first stop of the tour was the Kremlin. On the way, Wade sensed a sudden Force-Ma-Jeure regarding his urinary tract. He worked his way to the back of the bus to use the facilities—locked. He was informed the head could not be used and would have to wait until they entered the Kremlin in about ten minutes. *Okay, fine.* A ten-minute wait would be uncomfortable but doable.

Wade's bus arrived in about ten minutes along with the seven other tour buses. Now he had to piss so bad his molars broke into a chorus of "Anchors Aweigh." It was getting to be decision time: does he piss in his pants or on the Kremlin lawn? Panic was beginning to set in as he searched his fanny pack for a piece of string or a rubber band. To make a long story shorter, he did make it. However, by the time he achieved relief, the group had moved on. He finally found them, so all's well that ends well. The Kremlin seemed to be one big museum spread out in many buildings, like the Smithsonian in Washington, DC.

Wade's not big on museums, but he was impressed with what he saw. The tour of the Kremlin grounds and buildings consumed the next three hours.

The next item on the agenda was lunch in what the tour guide said was an opera house, also part of the Kremlin. The meal started with a salad and continued with a bowl of borscht, beef stroganoff, French fries, and an ice-cream log for dessert. For drinks, there was a choice of bottled water, a cabernet wine circa 1995, and a beverage referred to as coffee; mud would be a better term. All things considered, it was a very good meal.

The next stop was forty-five minutes at and around Red Square to sightsee, shop, or whatever. Wade was surprised at the diminutive size of Red Square. From the TV news stories, he expected a much larger area.

The tour finished off with a tour of the city and a final stop for last-minute souvenir shopping. The police joined the group at their last stop to escort the eight-bus caravan through and around traffic back to the airport. The unexpected events that followed dictated a need for the escort. Police escorts were also required from the ship to the St. Petersburg airport and from the Moscow airport to the Kremlin. These escorts were a real big help. For a supposedly poor country, there are a *lot* of vehicles.

To make matters worse, an accident had traffic backed up for miles in both directions. As if that wasn't bad enough, a car hit the bus. So there the bus sat while the bus driver and the auto driver tried to work out a financial arrangement for the damage to the bus.

The tour guide told everyone this is standard practice in Moscow.

About a half hour into negotiations, a police car showed up. A decision was made. Since the driver of the car didn't have enough money to pay for the damages, the police officer confiscated the offender's driver's license and had his vehicle pushed off the highway.

While all this was going on, the original police escort was long gone, along with the other tour buses. Police officer number two assumed escort duties—a fortuitous resolution to the problem since traffic was jammed up tighter than Toby's ass.

The accident occurred just prior to entering the on-ramp. Nobody was prepared for what happened next.

The police officer guided their bus and the following three buses, one lane at a time, into the left lane of the oncoming highway traffic. That's right, they were now in the fast lane of oncoming traffic. Even more surprised had to be the oncoming drivers seeing a line of buses approaching head-on. Watching the drivers make for the right lanes was comical, to say the least. This continued for about two miles until they caught up to the buses that had left them earlier. With them back in the convoy, the eight buses continued the wrong way in the fast lane of oncoming cars. The police officer then stopped the oncoming traffic for all lanes so they could exit the highway onto a frontage road that ran parallel to the highway. The caravan continued on this route for another mile or so until it passed the original accident. Now it was a simple matter of stopping eight lanes of traffic (four lanes each way) allowing the buses to reenter the main highway for smooth sailing to the airport. A sigh of relief resonated throughout the bus as the passengers realized that the performance of an extremely "take charge" police officer eliminated the need to spend the night in Moscow.

Except for a very slow-moving line at the airport security gate and a half-hour wait on the tarmac, waiting to take off, the trek back to the ship continued smoothly.

The Lone Sailor

Enlistment in the Navy is in his future.
Not just a job, it's an adventure.
The Lone Sailor

Nine weeks of training he hopes to survive.
Lessons learned may keep him alive.
The Lone Sailor

His training now complete,
It's time for him to join the fleet.
The Lone Sailor

Moored alongside the pier, his home
        of steel construction,
From keel to superstructure, a vessel
        of peace or destruction.

The command is given to get underway.
The ship eases from the quay.

Leaving port, passing ships of gray,
For all who serve, fair winds and
        following seas, he prays.
The Lone Sailor

One of many who keep our country free,
The next nine months he will spend at sea.
The Lone Sailor

He's a resident of a floating city,
A chaplain to keep him in touch
        with God almighty.
The Lone Sailor

When on liberty in the various ports,
He is an ambassador of the highest sort.
The Lone Sailor

The bow now points towards the States.
The cruise nearly over, he can hardly wait.
The Lone Sailor

The families stand on the pier with
        anticipation and glee,
Their loved ones home from the sea.

With his wallet stocked with a
        great deal of money,
He frequents the pubs in search of a honey.
The Lone Sailor

All the Proper Steps

My eyes were open; however, their focusing mechanism acted like a camera lens in the hands of an amateur photographer. The surroundings roamed from fuzzy to adequate several times before settling on adequate.

Everything was white. The walls were white. The beds were white. The ceiling was white. The only thing not white was me. I was one long red skid mark broken by patches of black and blue.

Where am I? Am I dead? Is this heaven? If I am in heaven, it's going to be a short stay. Angels are not allowed to think my thoughts.

And then she appeared: a goddess. She made Aphrodite look like a bag lady. Her angelic countenance was framed by long silky blonde hair and deep blue eyes. Breasts that deserved a crisp salute as they passed in review, and a waist that Dolly Parton would envy. Calves that made me curse the hemline of her white starched uniform because it spoiled my view of her legs that stretched from here to there. As she floated toward me, I could only envision what had to be a delightful heart-shaped derriere that moved like a paint shaker at Home Depot.

She must have sensed my ogling. I told myself not to be so crude and chauvinistic, but I had never listened to myself in the past, so why start now?

"Well, you finally decided to join us," she purred. The words rolled from her mouth slowly, seductively. I had a sudden desire for a lip sandwich.

"Is there anything I can do for you?" she asked.

With a numb mind and a quick mouth, I said, "Join me for a trip to some secluded island for champagne and caviar."

She laughed but said, "No."

Undaunted, I asked if she would settle for some serious fooling around. Another negative reply, but at least she paused before answering.

I was wearing her down.

Just as I was about to ask her another lewd question, she was paged. I watched her little heart-shaped fanny bounce away.

The old man in the bed next to me rolled over, faced me, and said, "Nice try,

Sonny, but I gotta tell ya, you didn't have a chance in a million with her."

"Well, Pop, I figure I had a fifty-fifty chance. She could have said yes. And my name isn't Sonny, it's Duke."

The old man and I chatted for a while. During our conversation, Ben told me about his operation, and I told him about my motorcycle accident, at least all that I could remember. In the next half hour or so, we solved all the problems of the world. With those out of the way, we decided to get some rest.

I eased back, stared at the ceiling, and thought of Dawn. The name fit her perfectly. Watching her was tantamount to watching the sunrise of a new day, bringing with it hope, dreams, and new frontiers to challenge and conquer. She reentered the ward, and my blood pressure surpassed the two-hundred mark.

As Dawn passed Ben, he let out a sigh, and his head flopped to one side. With the grace and agility of a jungle cat, she was at his side instantly. She turned his head toward the ceiling, placed her ear on Ben's chest, and listened for a heartbeat—nothing. She turned her cheek to his mouth, hoping to feel his breath against her face—again, nothing. Dawn raised her right arm and delivered a sharp blow to Ben's chest. She then placed the heel of her left hand at the base of his sternum. With her right hand on top of her left hand, fingers interlocked, she began the rhythmic count of fifteen chest depressions to two lung-filling breaths.

Ben's eyes opened in amazement. In slow, jerky sentences, he grunted, "I…wish…you…wouldn't…do…that. I…can't…breathe…when…you…do…that."

Poor Ben never fell asleep again while Dawn was on duty.

Learn or Burn

The building was old, charred, and covered with soot. Some would say that a concrete structure possessing all of these unsightly characteristics would be of little or no value to anyone. Some would, but not the thirty instructors and untold number of students who have employed its services as a training facility. This was one of the thoughts going through my mind as the primer-gasoline inched its way across the surface of the twelve hundred gallons of diesel fuel that lay in the bilges of the engine room mock-up.

Forty-five students were dressed in rain gear on a sunny afternoon, waiting to enter the mock-up. I looked to my left. Charlie and Sam, the rear and center doors hose team instructors, gave me their thumbs-up signal of readiness. I then looked to my right. Tom, the forward door hose team instructor, also gave me a sign, but it wasn't a thumb he was extending; he was a couple of fingers off. I returned his obscene gesture with a smile and pushed the button.

As usual, the explosion caught the students' attention. Flames shot out of the doors fifteen feet, resembling a three-headed fire-breathing monster. Slowly the flames drew back, licking the sides of the building, then receded inside as the exhaust fans gained momentum.

"I've never seen it do that before," Tom shouted.

"Me neither, I think I'm scared," Charlie replied.

The explosion is designed as an attention-getter, the jocular dialogue as a fear retardant. Both are very effective.

Two minutes had elapsed since the light-off. The high-temperature alarm sounded, indicating the inside temperature reached one-thousand-plus degrees Fahrenheit.

"What are you waiting for?" Tom asked impatiently. "Blow the damn whistle." I just looked at him and smiled. Tom remembered the finger gesture and said, "Okay, you made your point."

I blew the damn whistle.

All three hose teams moved up simultaneously, working their hoses up and down, forcing the flames further into the structure.

With the teams at their respective doors, I blew the whistle again. We moved in, hoses now sweeping side to side. Clouds of steam formed as the cold water came in contact with the hot steel floor grates. The steam intensified the discomfort already experienced by the heat and smoke.

To my left, I heard a student screaming, "I can't see! I can't see!"

"Don't worry," Sam said. "I know where we're going, just follow me."

Another student piped up, "I can't breathe. I've gotta get outta here."

"You're talking, you're breathing," Charlie said as he tightened his grip on the student's rain parka. Charlie was an experienced instructor, and his experience told him the man was getting ready to bail out. He also knew bailing out was contagious and could not be permitted.

The second explosion was completely unexpected. Fire engulfed the hose teams.

One man lost his balance and fell to the floor. In seconds, the hot grating and flames penetrated his rain gear. He leaped to his feet as if jabbed by a cattle prod.

Unfortunately, the seriousness of the situation stifled the humor of the scene.

Concussion from the blast lifted one man, who weighed about one hundred pounds, and deposited him twelve feet from where he had been standing. He would have soared farther had the adjacent building not stopped him in mid-flight. Shaken but unharmed, he staggered to a safe area.

Charlie, Sam, and Tom quickly gained control of the situation. Hoses were manned, and we were back in action. I sounded three whistle blasts, the signal to move back to the doors.

With the teams at their respective doors, I had a decision to make. Do we back all the way out and extinguish the fire with the built-in sprinkler system? Or do we reengage the fire?

It was no contest: Our motto is *learn or burn.*

Loudmouths and Lines

Larry sat on the edge of his bunk. It was 4:30 a.m. He reached for a cigarette, lit it, and cursed the day he had started smoking. He justified his habit by telling himself it was keeping his weight down, which was a good thing as he already weighed 230-plus pounds. As he sat there, smoking his cigarette, allowing the fuzziness of sleep to clear his brain, his thoughts drifted back in time.

It was one o'clock in the morning when the bus passed through the gates of the Naval Training Center, San Diego, California. On the bus were eighty very apprehensive young men of varied backgrounds and cultures, who, like Larry, were recent high school graduates.

The bus stopped in front of an old wooden building that, judging from its appearance, must have been built during World War I.

Larry was relieved that the day that had begun nineteen hours earlier was over, and he would soon be getting some much-needed sleep.

The man who entered the bus was in his thirties and looked as though he had just stepped out of a men's salon. As the man bellowed orders to the busload of new arrivals, Larry's apprehension turned to fear. Having led a sheltered life, he was not accustomed to all of this yelling.

"All right, you bunch of clowns, off the bus and fall in as directed." Everyone piled out of the bus and stood on his assigned number that was painted in the small square on a patio alongside the bus. The man continued barking instructions: "That number you clowns are standing on is your billet number. For the next week of processing, you do not have a name, only a billet number." The decibel level of the person barking out the instructions caused Larry to surmise this guy must have learned to whisper in a sawmill.

Filling out a countless number of forms cost Larry and his traveling companions two more hours of precious sleep.

Larry leaped from a sound-asleep prone position to a wide-awake position of attention in a microsecond, a feat he had never experienced before and one he had no desire to repeat.

The disgusting sound that had so rudely awakened Larry was a nightstick being rotated along the corrugated inside circumference of a fifty-five-gallon garbage can, coupled with some loudmouth screaming, "Reveille, reveille, off your hocks and grab your socks, reveille!"

In another step in the five-day processing, Larry and fifty-nine others were once again formed into another of the endless lines. They were now standing naked in a long line, in billet number order. Larry realized there was a definite flaw in the axiom that started, "All men are created equal."

The line was for a routine hernia check, but something looked wrong. It took Larry a couple of minutes to figure out what it was that did not look quite right. When he did, a vile taste filled his mouth. The doctor was sitting at a small table with the recruits' medical forms stacked in front of him. As each recruit approached, the doctor would shove his finger into the recruit's scrotum and tell him to cough. The doctor would then lick his finger and use it to turn the page.

One recruit was told he had a loose urethra ring. The quick-thinking recruit asked, "Do you think I need a valve job too, doc?" The recruit was ordered to do one hundred push-ups. It was obvious to the rest of us that the doctor had no sense of humor.

"Don't these lines ever end?" Larry asked the recruit in front of him. It was afternoon, and the day had been one line after the other.

"I don't think so," the recruit answered.

"What's this line for?" Larry asked more for the purpose of starting a conversation than for curiosity. Upon hearing the answer, mixed feelings of pain and terror caused him to shudder. "We're going to get a shot with a square needle in the left what?"

One night, Larry was walking his post, guarding, of all things, a clothesline. As he walked, he pondered the procedure for challenging intruders. "Halt, who is there?" Upon response, he would command the person to advance and be recognized. If the person checked out, Larry would let them pass.

Someone or something approached. Larry shouted, "Halt, who goes there?"

"Captain Marvel," the person replied.

"Yeah, and I'm Superman. Fly your ass over here to be recognized."

Larry marched his two-hour punishment tour, cursing himself for not studying the chain of command information sheet. There really was a "Captain Marvel."

The sound of a car horn jarred Larry back to the present. He extinguished his cigarette, grabbed his towel and toilet articles, and headed for the shower.

It was 5:00 a.m., Larry entered the room, switched on the lights, rattled the garbage with his nightstick, and screamed, "Reveille, reveille, off your hocks and grab your socks, reveille!"

Promises

"One .38 caliber revolver, one holster, one belt, one shore patrol armband, and four .38-caliber shells. You're all set to go out and get the bad guys," said the man issuing my equipment.

"Four shells—now I know how Barney Fife felt," I mumbled to myself as I left the armory. I took consolation in the fact that I was three shells ahead of Barney.

The police car arrived at 7:00 p.m. I climbed in, and we were off to "protect and serve."

"My name is George Sanders, but everyone calls me Sandy," the cop said as we pulled away.

"Okay, Sandy, call me Ski."

"First time on shore patrol?" he asked.

"No, but it's my first time riding with the police."

During our get-acquainted conversation, Sandy asked me if the Navy was still issuing only four shells. When I answered in the affirmative, he told me to get a couple out of the glove compartment.

"How much do I owe you?" I asked.

"Nothing," he replied. "They're police reloads kept mainly for target practice and as spares for the officers who use the standard, police-issued .38."

I noticed his gun was definitely not standard issue: I had seen elephant guns with smaller bores. He told me the gun was new on the market: a .44-four caliber magnum. I guess he thought he was Clint Eastwood.

The first couple of hours were spent conducting routine building security checks, with only one interruption for a speeder. The driver would have gotten off with only a warning, but he turned belligerent, so Sandy presented him with a citation for sixty-three in a fifty-five zone. "It seems they never learn," Sandy said as we continued our patrol.

Sandy was thirty-five, single, and in his fourteenth year on the force. Compared to him, I was still wet behind the ears at the tender age of twenty-two, and with only four years of Naval service.

"With those chubby, pink cheeks, does anyone call you 'Porky?'" I asked.

"Not more than once," he replied.

The long silent police radio came to life. "All units, be on the lookout for a 1961 Cadillac, white over blue, Virginia license

143628. Vehicle reported stolen within the past two hours."

As we waited for the light to change, a brace of very well-proportioned redheaded persons of the female persuasion jiggled across our path.

"Would you?" Sandy asked.

"Are you kidding? I'd crawl over a mile of broken beer bottles just to smell the exhaust from the laundry truck that carried their undies."

Watching the young ladies almost caused us to miss the Cadillac that also crossed our path.

"What do you say we check him out?" Sandy asked. "We might get lucky."

"Okay, but I would much rather get lucky with the redheads," I replied.

By the time the light changed and we caught up to the Caddy, we were out of town.

Sandy turned on the red lights, but the driver of the Cadillac either did not see the lights or chose to ignore them. Sandy then hit the siren. Again, no response—it was as if we did not exist. Sandy paralleled the car, and I yelled at the driver to pull over. The driver, a young man in his early twenties, acted very nonchalant. He just glanced in my direction, pulled off the road, and stopped.

Following standard procedure, I called dispatch, informed them that we had stopped the stolen car, and gave them our location.

Sandy said, "Okay, Ski, you go get him and bring him back here. I'll stay in the car in case he decides to take off again."

I was a bit dubious, to say the least, and terrified to say the most. I drew my weapon and got out of the car.

Either the man was very fast or I was very slow or both—I'm not sure. However, I was sure of one thing: I had been shot.

The bullet creased my left arm, causing a stinging sensation as I dove for cover.

It's funny how the mind works. As I was diving for cover, I thought of all those westerns and how the hero would say, "I'm okay, it's only a flesh wound." In reality, I was saying, "Flesh wound, my ass, it hurts."

I hit the ground on my right shoulder, almost losing my weapon. I rolled over twice, ending up on my belly with a mouthful of grass. I spat it out and wondered how cows could possibly eat this stuff. I fired two shots, missing the gunman, as he took cover behind the Caddy's door.

Noticing the weeds I was lying in were not providing me with adequate cover, I surveyed the area for something better. Looking around, I heard Sandy talking on the radio. I hoped he was calling for backup. We needed all the help we could muster.

I decided to ask for help myself. "Lord, get me out of this, and I promise to give up drinking, loose women, and I'll go to church every Sunday."

A puff of dirt erupted by my foot, and I heard the twang of the bullet as it ricocheted into the woods. I took aim and fired my weapon three times in rapid succession. One slug hit air, the other two slammed into the Caddy—my aim was improving.

My heart was pounding with the ferocity of a wrecking ball in the hands of a crazed demolitions expert.

On my left, and slightly to my rear, I heard three cannon blasts; it was Sandy and his elephant gun. One round pierced the door on the suspect's left, one round penetrated the door on the suspect's right, and the third buried itself in the dirt between his feet. Each time Sandy fired, the recoil caused his arms to rise slightly. He brought the weapon down for another shot, but the gunman, noticing one left, one right, and one low, must have decided that Sandy had him zeroed in because he threw his gun down and assumed a spread-eagle position on the ground.

After receiving his rights, the gunman confessed not only to the stolen car but also to a liquor store holdup.

Leaving the hospital, Sandy asked, "What do you say to stopping off and having a couple of cold ones? We might even run into those two redheads again."

"Why not?" I answered. "After all, tomorrow's Sunday. We can sleep late."

The Good Samaritan

Wade, weary and confused, crawled into his bunk that balmy August evening. He lay on his back, head resting in the palms of his clasped hands, staring at the ceiling and thinking about the morning's events. One question ran through his mind over and over again: *Why me, Lord? I've been good.*

The morning had begun with a beam of sunlight that woke Wade from a restful night's sleep. He got out of bed, walked to the mirror, and admired his reflected handsome features. After saying good morning to himself, he shaved, showered, and dressed for breakfast. He downed breakfast with the gusto of a hound dog, said his goodbyes, and was on the road with the satisfaction of getting an early start.

Wisconsin's beautiful scenery was only enhanced by the sight of a mother doe and her fawn bounding across the open field alongside the road. Wade's thoughts drifted back to the many times he had been deer hunting without seeing a deer. He wondered if, because of their grace and beauty, he would have been able to shoot a buck had he seen one.

His thoughts more on the deer than on driving caused him to make the wrong turn at the intersection. Realizing his mistake, Wade scanned the area for a place to turn around. The shoulder of the road was sandy, but he saw tire tracks and reasoned it was worth a try. As the rear tires of the van spun themselves deeper and deeper into the sand, Wade realized he had made a dumb decision.

Wade got out of the vehicle in order to survey his dilemma. The front of the trailer had plowed into the sand, and the van's rear tires were buried so deep that the differential housing was resting on the sandy soil, a condition that provided the same effect as jacking up the rear end as though one were about to change both tires simultaneously.

Wade's next step was to plan a course of action that would relieve his present situation and put him back on the road.

Plan "A" involved shouting obscenities and kicking the tires. This action was not only ineffective; it caused pain to his pedal digits. Adding to his frustration was the parade of lookie-loos who slowed down to observe his dilemma and chuckled as they resumed speed.

What seemed like hours later, a car sped by, slowed, turned around, and drove back.

"Need help?" the driver asked.

Wade's first thought was to say, "No, I have the mineral rights to this spot, and I am digging for gold." However, discretion being the better part of valor, he replied with a simple, "Yes."

The Good Samaritan was a young man in his early twenties. He introduced himself as Sam. He had a big black Labrador retriever with him that jumped out of Sam's car and romped off into the woods.

With the small talk out of the way, Sam informed Wade he had plenty of experience in these situations and asked Wade if he had a jack.

Plan B was simple but time-consuming. They would jack up the rear end of the van, fill in the holes left by the tires, push the van sideways, letting it drop to the ground. This procedure would be repeated until the rear tires contacted solid ground. The idea was brilliant except for one small detail: there was no solid ground in the immediate area. Unfortunately, that fact was not realized until forty-five minutes of drudgery.

Meanwhile, the dog returned from his romp in the woods, dropped down, resting his head on his front paws, watching Sam and Wade. Wade said, "Look at your dog. He's probably thinking we look like two cub bears trying to do a number on a greasy football while wearing boxing gloves."

Sam laughed and said, "You're probably right."

Undaunted, and with the dog looking on, the determined pair moved on to plan C. They removed the floorboards from the trailer, jacked up the rear end of the van, placed the floorboards under the tires, let the rear end down, started up the engine, put it in gear, and gave 'er hell. When the spinning tires left the boards, two rooster tails of sand grew behind the van, and in seconds, the van was on the blacktop. It worked so well, Wade and Sam couldn't figure out why they hadn't thought of the idea earlier.

With the trailer hauled back up to the road and hitched to the van, it was time to put the floorboards back and reload the motorcycle.

Wade said, "Well, at least we can drive the motorcycle back to the road." Wrong again—the engine wouldn't start. Luckily, the motorcycle was fairly easy to push.

Ten minutes later, everything was loaded, latched down, and stowed.

After a couple of beers, the "thank-yous," and "you're welcomes," Wade went his way and Sam his.

Yes, it was quite a day, Wade thought. It reminded him of the trailer tire episode, but that's another story.

Pirate's Week

The plane touched down on schedule at Owen Roberts International Airport on the island of Grand Cayman. The airport is named after Owen Roberts, British Royal Air Force (RAF) Wing Commander Owen Roberts.

Grand Cayman is the largest of the three islands that make up the Caymans: Grand Cayman, Little Cayman, and Cayman Brac. The islands are sometimes erroneously referred to as "The Grand Caymans." The capital of Grand Cayman is George Town.

Frank's enthusiasm grew in proportion to the upcoming ten days of diving and Pirate's Week celebration. This would be his first organized dive adventure since acquiring his certification card, or C card. Pirate's Week started in the early 1980s. Pirate's Week is a Cayman Islands festival celebrating the history of Grand Cayman, at one time a favorite haunt for pirates and buccaneers. The entire island is transformed into a pirate encampment for the week-long festival. There is a mock invasion of George Town, parades, pageants, and the trial of the pirates. Everyone dresses up in costumes, and the singing, dancing, and food fairs that are held throughout the island all revolve around a pirate theme.

The group consisted of twenty-some divers ranging from their early twenties to middle fifties, with singles, married couples, and "just friends."

The first obstacle to the week of fun and frolic was customs. Customs has never been accused of breaking the sound barrier, and the pace in Grand Cayman ranges from slow to slower to slowest. If one of the residents notices aggravation in someone's expression, they just say, "You on Cayman time, mon." The sooner the American tourist learns this, the less chance he will have of developing an ulcer, and the sooner he will relax.

One in the group named Bill would be considered the class clown and, if taken seriously, would be considered just plain rude and obnoxious. An example of this is when he turned to the couple behind him and asked, "So are you guys married or just shacking up?" He continued to act up, and it wasn't long before the airport police apprehended him and escorted him away to the cheers and applause of the other passengers. Then irony rose from the ashes. The police escorted Bill right through customs and immigration. As everyone exited the airport, there was Bill, sitting in the shade, knocking down rum punches and asking what took everyone so long.

The group arrived at Plantation Village, their home for the next ten days. They were divided, four to a room. Frank's roommates were Tom and Sam from Los Angeles and George from Las Vegas, as was Frank.

With bedroom assignments determined and gear unpacked, it was time for nourishment and libations. Frank heard the ladies leaving the adjoining room. He grabbed a cookie, and as they passed, he conjured up his best lecherous voice and asked, "Chocolate chip cookie, little girls?" They smiled and continued their journey. "Drat!"

A restaurant close to the condos was picked, and off went the quartet of the newly acquainted. This is when Frank was introduced to a mollusk called conch. When Frank pronounced the word as spelled, the rest of the group laughed, and the waiter promptly corrected him. The waiter said the correct pronunciation in the Caymans was "konk." Conch is served in many ways, but the most popular is conch salad and conch fritters. Frank opted for an appetizer plate of fritters.

Back at the condo, Frank was sitting on the veranda, sipping a rum and Coke, and enjoying the serenity while listening to the waves lapping on the shoreline. Suddenly, a scream of pain pierced the silence. A few of the group decided on a night snorkel. Unfortunately, one of the snorkelers swam into a school of jellyfish. He was taken to the hospital for treatment. The doctors were able to relieve the pain. However, welts covering most of his upper body would remain for months.

Frank woke early, which was his nature when sleeping in new surroundings. Being first up, he brewed a pot of coffee and walked out to the balcony. He heard a woman's voice coming from one of the bedrooms. He thought his ears were playing tricks because a woman was not assigned to their room. Mystery solved—George found a companion. Frank made the decision to follow and observe George while taking copious notes on how to pick up women.

The dive boat arrived on schedule, and the happy campers were en route to their first of two dive sites. The dive boat was a converted WWII landing craft seen in any war movie when the troops are making their assault on the beach.

A COMPILATION OF SHORT STORIES

DIVE PRECHECK

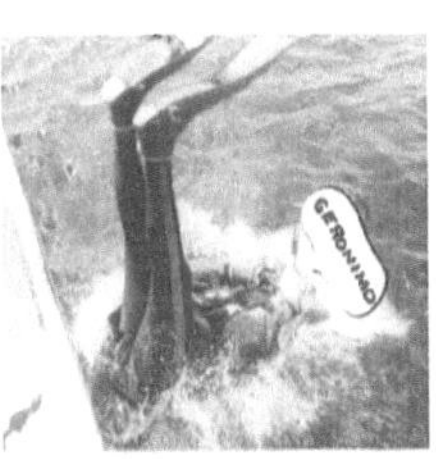

The standard procedure for diving is deepest dive first and shallower dive second. The first dive profile was one hundred feet for twenty minutes. For some unknown reason, Frank used air at an unexpected rate. He tapped his dive buddy on the shoulder and indicated his tank was down to 500 psi. Jack nodded and swam to the dive master, letting him know the pair would be heading to the surface. By the time Jack returned, Frank sucked the last breath of air—his tank was dry. A hundred feet below the surface is not a good place to be without air. Frank gave the "out-of-air, need-to-buddy-breathe" signal.

Most divers have a spare regulator called an octopus. Jack didn't see the need for one when he bought his regulator—a situation he would rectify at his first opportunity.

The pair made the slow ascent to the surface. The second dive was a routine fifty-foot dive that proceeded without a hitch.

The divers were in for a treat—a third dive. The dive boat eased into a cove and dropped anchor. The dive master yelled, "Suit up, the pool is open!"

Frank looked over the side and was confused. *Where is the coral? The depth is less than fifteen feet, and the bottom is nothing but sand and weeds.* But he also figured, *What the hell—a dive is a dive.*

Minutes after entering the water, fifteen to twenty stingrays arrived. They were like puppy dogs, interacting with the divers and looking for a handout. Frank thought, *This could be my best dive.* Originally, fishermen would enter the cove to clean their catch. It didn't take long for the stingrays to take advantage of a free and easy meal.

On the way back to town, the alarm was sounded: "Man your battle stations."

Battle stations? What battle stations? Another dive boat flying the Jolly Roger was attacking. Ammunition of choice consisted of water balloons propelled using a three-person slingshot. Frank's group was outmanned and outgunned. To save face, the decision was made to outclass the attackers. Frank and several others manned the rail and mooned the crew of the attacking boat. *Let them try to get that image out of their heads prior to dozing off tonight, or better still, at suppertime.*

That evening, most of the group met at the Holiday Inn hotel for dancing, drinking, and rehashing the day's events. The Holiday Inn was chosen because of Barefoot Man. He came to the island several years earlier and literally sang for his supper and a hammock on the beach. Over the years, he graduated from a solo act to form a small band that played anywhere they could find a gig.

Barefoot writes most of his own music, which can be thought of as naughty or nice depending on the listener's point of view. A lot of his lyrics are double entendre in nature. An example would be the song that tells the story of a honeymooning couple and the gentleman in the adjoining room. He hears the husband tell his bride, "I am the husband, you get on top."

To which the wife replies, "I am the wife, you get on top."

The husband says, "We will both get on top."

Now the man next door had to see this, so he bent down and peeked into the keyhole. The honeymooners were trying to close a suitcase.

Frank and a couple of others were sipping drinks and talking about the day's events when Sharon strolled up to the group. Sharon is a statuesque blond and a not-too-former Miss Nevada. She pointed to Frank and said, "You, dance floor, now."

Frank morphed from a pudgy, gray-haired middle-aged man to a young Paul Newman, even if it was in his own mind. As Frank tried to move to the beat of the music without stepping on or over his own two feet, he noticed the confused look on some of the other men on the dance floor. They had to be asking themselves, *Why is she with him?*

Frank looked back with a cat-that-ate-the-canary grin, stifling the urge to yell, "Eat your heart out!"

The rest of the week was diving, fighting off attacking dive boats, shopping, snorkeling, drinking, eating, and dancing.

As the wheels of the Cayman Airlines jet lifted off the tarmac, Frank sat back in his seat and said to himself, "I'll be back."

About the Author

To paraphrase someone or other: A funny thing happened on the journey to writing this book: *I aged.* Go figure.

I graduated high school on a Friday night in June of 1955, enlisted in the United States Navy on Monday morning, and within six days of my eighteenth birthday, I arrived at the Naval Training Center in San Diego, California, listening to a lot of people yelling at me. What's a billet number? And why do I have to stand on it?

I spent the next twenty years traveling the world with Uncle Sam as my travel agent. A few years later, I moved to Las Vegas and worked in the convention industry for another twenty years.

I am now fully retired and spend my time researching destinations in the hope of viewing the world through a windshield.

9 798893 089042